T0131881

Marcus' New Adventure

Tinika Wyatt

Art by Aliyah Sidqe

This is a work of fiction. All of the characters, names, incidents, organizations, and dialogue in this novel are either the products of the author's imagination or are used fictitiously.

WestBow Press books may be ordered through booksellers or by contacting:

WestBow Press
A Division of Thomas Nelson & Zondervan
1663 Liberty Drive
Bloomington, IN 47403
www.westbowpress.com
844-714-3454

Interior Image Credit: Aliyah Sidqe

Scripture quotations are taken from the Holy Bible, New Living Translation, copyright ©1996, 2004, 2015 by Tyndale House Foundation. Used by permission of Tyndale House Publishers, Carol Stream, Illinois 60188. All rights reserved.

ISBN: 978-1-6642-2463-6 (sc)
ISBN: 978-1-6642-2464-3 (e)

Library of Congress Control Number: 2021903307

Print information available on the last page.

WestBow Press rev. date: 03/31/2021

WESTBOW
PRESS®
A DIVISION OF THOMAS NELSON
& ZONDERVAN

Marcus' New Adventure

On a quiet neighborhood street
Where trees and sunshine meet
There lived an adventurous boy
Named Marcus

In his perfect little world
Where he, mom, dad and baby girl
Lived happily all together
Life was perfect

Dad was his best friend
Mom loved him to no end
And baby sister
Well, she was kind of a princess

But his imagination was king
He could do almost anything
From far-away lands
Back to his kitchen

He could play and dream
Defeat dragons who were mean
Fight bad guys
And always be the hero

There was nothing too scary
No hairy bear too hairy
'Cause Marcus was brave
With no worries

Till one day mom was crying
Dad yelled "this isn't working"
The life Marcus had
Started crumbling

His parents wanted to live apart
Mom said she had a broken heart
And no matter what Marcus tried
He couldn't fix it

He made sure to clean his room
Took better care of baby June
Even picked up all his toys
But it wasn't helping

Before long they were moving
Leaving dad behind and lonely
Off to grandma's and grandpa's
To stay awhile

Marcus liked his grandparents
But didn't want to live in their basement
Didn't want to leave his friends
His school and neighborhood

And what about dad
He must be very sad
Without his best friend
Named Marcus

Mom was no better
She'd burst into tears if you let her
Marcus didn't understand
Why they had to

Live in separate spaces
Go to different places
No more family dinners, picnics
Or game nights

No dad AND mom
Just dad OR mom
This new adventure
Drove Marcus wild

So what was he to do
In a new house, a new school
Where this new world
Was so very different

Seeing dad just once a week
Was barely enough time to speak
And tell dad everything he learned
Liked and hated

He wanted to share his new world
Even more, put things back the way they were
Dad and mom holding hands
Making kissy faces

Dad explained that wouldn't happen
Put Marcus on his lap and
Gave him the biggest hug
He had ever had

"I love you from the ground to the sky
You're forever my favorite little guy"
Dad told Marcus
With tears

He needed to know dad was still the same
Even though everything else had changed
At least that made things
Not so bad

He knew this new adventure
Would be his toughest villain
But mom 's love and dad's assurance
Would keep him strong

Plus, he had special powers
Grandparents who spent hours
Making him laugh, letting him cry
Just being with him

Grandpa was like dad but much older
He told weird jokes and had hairy shoulders
He loved playing catch, wrestling
And taught Marcus math

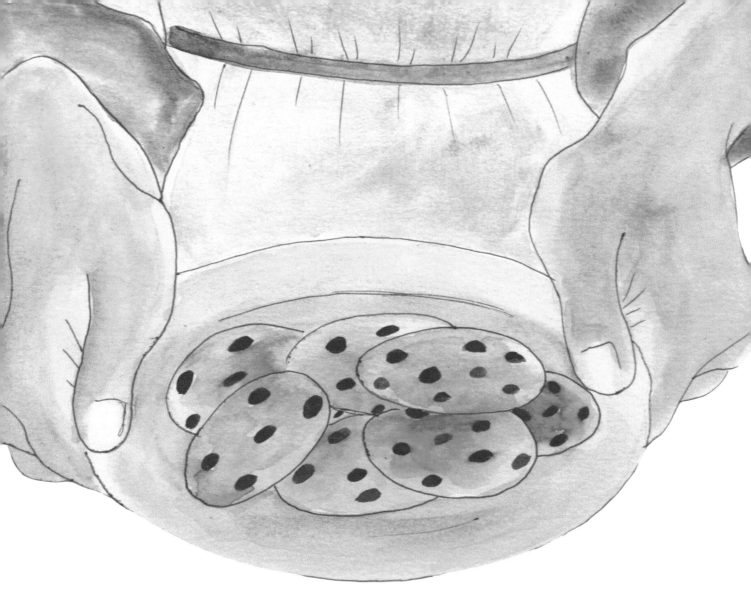

Grandma baked cookies and cakes
She loved kisses and squeezing June's face
She was the sweetest old lady
Marcus ever met

But they had a few rules
Marcus didn't think were cool
Mom agreed it might be good
To try new things

No running in the house
No jumping on the couch
Muddy shoes left outside
On the back patio

Church every Sunday
Interrupted Marcus' fun day
But snacks and games
He could get used to

He actually liked his shiny church shoes
Hearing what they called good news
About God's love and His Son
Named Jesus

God created the entire world
Every animal, every boy and girl
He had never heard
This amazing creation story

He learned God has a plan for him
Jesus even died for him
So, He would take care of
Dad, mom and baby June

He was told he could talk to God
Anytime, anywhere and be honest
So, he told Him everything
Even all the bad stuff

Marcus began saying his prayers
Grandma told him Jesus really cared
So he prayed for many things
Especially mom's heart

Although his world was changing
And full of new strange things
It wasn't the worst
After all

Dad made the most of weekends
Mom was always there to tuck him in
His new school and teacher
Were okay too

Grandparents, neighbors
The mail man, the landscaper
Church members, everyone
Was so kind

They didn't know their smiles and hugs
Their pats and back rubs
Meant the world to a little boy
Uncertain

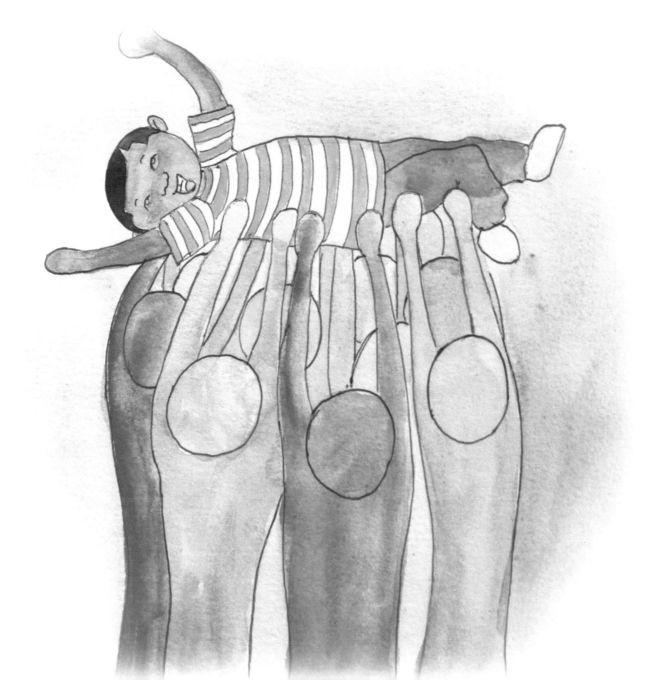

This story's ending isn't the happiest
But one a child can be happy in
Knowing he is surrounded
By love

Faith, hope and forgiveness
All part of this new adventure
To grow a beautiful boy
Named Marcus

Luke 12:7

And the very hairs on your head are all numbered. So don't be afraid; you are more valuable to God than a whole flock of sparrows.

1 Peter 5:7

Give all your worries and cares to God, for he cares about you.

Philippians 4:6

Don't worry about anything; instead, pray about everything. Tell God what you need, and thank him for all he has done.

Deuteronomy 31:6

Be strong and courageous! Do not be afraid and do not panic before them. For the LORD your God will personally go ahead of you. He will neither fail you nor abandon you.

Hebrews 13:5

"I will never fail you. I will never abandon you." -God

Printed in the United States
by Baker & Taylor Publisher Services